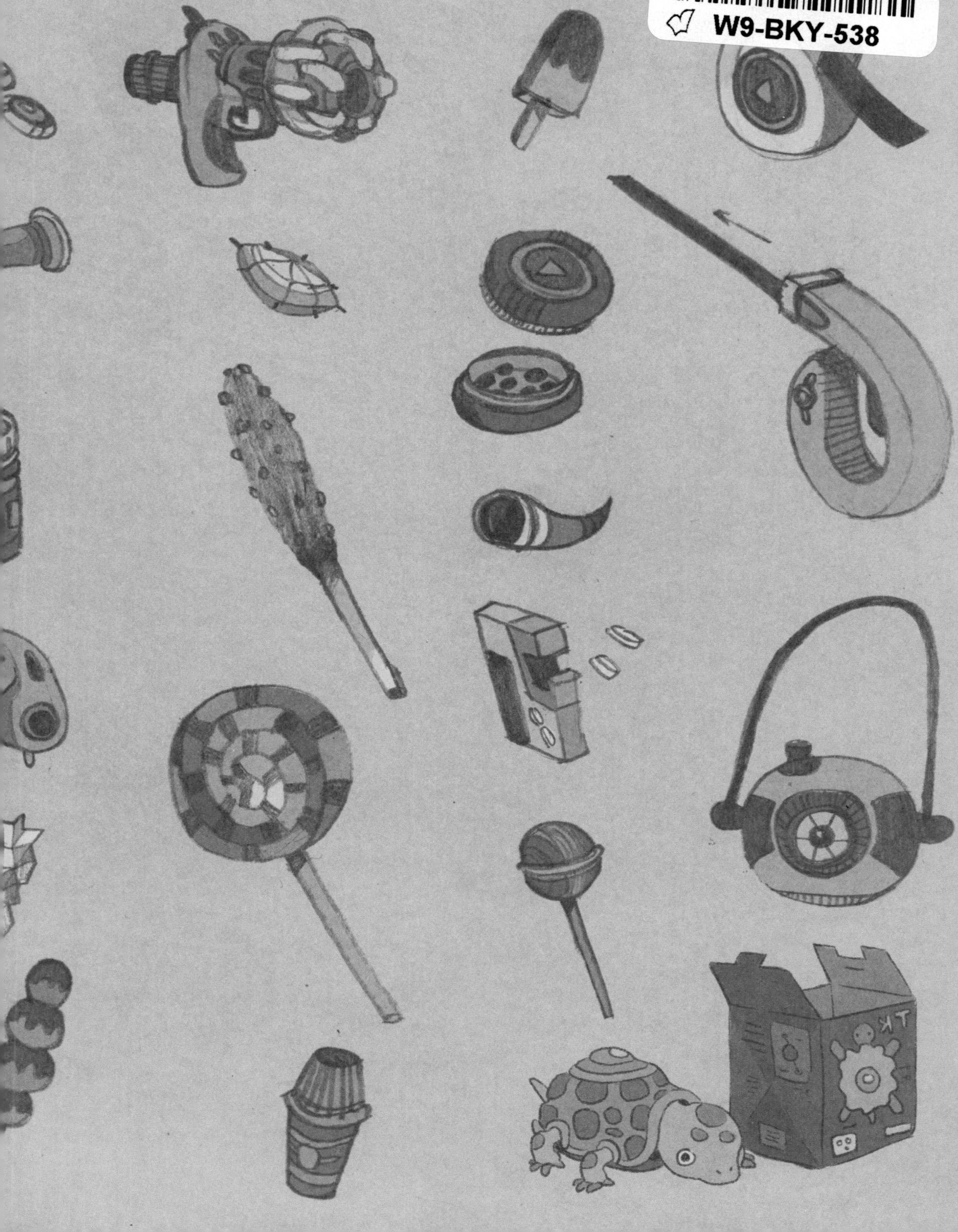
TK

DON'T SETTLE. SHOW YOUR METTLE!
GET A:
ZOOM DOG™!
NEW MODEL
Featuring HYPER-UBER-TOP-DRIVE™
GREAT FOR ALL KNIGHTS!
CHROME, SULFUR, HYDROGEN, YOU NAME IT*
* will not catalyze for Neon Knights
FLY TO THE SKY WITH A NE
FROGGIEPACK™
NEW and IMPROVED
CONTROL and SPEED and HANDLING
SATISFACTION GUARANTEED!!*
* Satisfaction not guaranteed for Neon Knights
RADIO REX
NEED REPAIRS? CALL BERYL!
ARE YOU THE LAST KNIGHT* WITHOUT A
MEOWPACK™?
INFINITE STORAGE!
WELL, WHAT ARE YOU WAITING FOR?
* OF COURSE, DON'T BOTHER IF YO
SPARKLE

CHASMA KNIGHTS

BOYA SUN
AND
KATE REED PETTY

:01
First Second
New York

To Mom and Dad

—Boya

To Clementine and Frances

—Kate

Everyone in the whole Chasma knows,
you catalyze Toys and your powers grow.
Your new Toys can schwoop and sizzle and glow!
(But ***Neon Knights*** can't. Their power's too low.)

Everyone in the whole Chasma can change,
whether chlorine or sulfur, your core is in range,
for the transforming Toys at the Toy Market exchange.
(But Neon Knights can't. They're ***very*** strange.)

Everyone in the whole Chasma goes through
six or eight Toys—in just one day or two.
Every time you get bored, you buy something ***new***!
(But Neon Knights ***can't***...)

CHAPTER 1: BERYL
...so what *can* they do?

SNIFF
SNIFF
WHOOOOSHHHH
!
PAH!

MEOW
Yup, a bronze Toy. And pretty good power!
BEEP
i've got ***oodles*** of toys.
PPFFT
bronze toys, chrome, nickel...
toys get thrown away ***all the time***.
but what i ***really*** need...
RRRRR

rrrrrRRR
...is a gold toy.
rrRRRRR

GOLD
Yes!
VROO
VROOOOO
Oh, no...

VRRO
VVVROOOOOOMM
VVOOOOMM
WHOP
ZIP!
SWING
VVRRROOOM

sulfur knights.
SULFUR!
COPPER!
ISOLATE!
SNAP!
SPLIT!
SEPARATE!

looks like they bought the new **zoomdogs**™...
...which **catalyze** just like the old ones.
show-offs.

Hey, Beryl.
SNIFF SNIFF
Whatcha *got* in there?
Looks like a buncha *junk*.
What do *you* want with all these Toys?
After all...

Everyone in the whole Chasma knows ***Neon Knights can't catalyze***.
They're all broken.
Broken toys for Broken Beryl.
Broken Beryl, Broken Beryl!

I'm *tired* of your teasing!
I don't *have* to catalyze!
I'm building something WAY MORE POWERFUL than what the *TOY MAKER*™ sells!
And then you'll be *sorry*!

HA HA HA HA HA HA
Ya hear that? Beryl thinks she's a TOY MAKER™?!
Listen, I'm sorry you're..."different."
But since you can't even catalyze a silly MEOWPACK™...

MEOW!?
WHOOP
HA!
Hey!
Let's go, Knights! The ***Toy Market*** is starting!
ARF!
GRRR

TOOT!
No, no, wait!
Grr
SULFUR!
COPPER!
RECOGNIZE!
MEET!
MERGE!
CATALYZE!
POOF

See ya round, Broken Beryl!
VRRRM
My gold Toy is in that MEOWPACK™!
it's okay. they'll get bored and throw it away.
VRRMM
I'll get it back.

HUFF
HUFF
HUFF
HUFF
TUT
TUT
TUT
TOY MARKET
TUT TUT
I wish *I* could fly.
CHEEP
CHEEP
CHEEP

CHEEP!
CHEEP!
CHEEP!
CHEEP!
All right, let's get that cat back!

TOY MARKET
ugh, i ***hate*** the toy market.
Go on, give it a try!
OOOOOO OOOOOHH
Watch ***this***!
AAAHH
oh.

it's coro.
CLAP
CLAP
CLAP
CLAP

everyone thinks she's so great.
because she's an ***oxygen knight***.
CLAP
CLAP
WOOOO!
YEAH!
"CORO"
that's the most ***powerful*** kind.
No, no, ***I'm*** nothing special...

You too can fly! It's the latest from the *Toy Maker™*, and it's compatible with *everyone*—speedy Sulfurs, nimble Nitrogens, I mean *everyone*!
AMAZING OCTO SPINNERR
OCTO SPINNER
As long as you're not a *Neon Knight*.
pft
HA HA HA
HA
More like Neon *Nobodies*!
HA-HA HA
HA HA
They're *very* strange.

OXYGEN, CHROME, RECOGNIZE!!
MEET, MERGE, CATALYZE!
POOF
Now, for my next demonstration!

The Whirligig!
FOOOSSHHHHHHHHH
Oh, no!
My MEOW-PACK™!

TOY
PUF
MEOW
SHOOOO
GET YOUR
tk
tk
tk

SHHOOOO
AH!
GET YOUR OWN
FFF
GASP!
GASP!
FFFF
FFFF

GET
OUR
OCTO SPINNER
CRASH!!
SALE
BAM!!
OCTO-SPINNER

Everything's *ruined*!
That's what you get for showing off!
Hi.
Um. That's... my MEOW-PACK™.
MEOW

my gold toy is still here.
phew.
Um. Need a hand?
No.

NNGGG
NNNGGG
HUFF
HUFF
Wow. Is this copper?

It's *junk* now. And I just bought it last month!
I've never seen copper with so much power still in it.
And who's going to buy all these dumb OCTOSPINNERS™ now?
BAM
How much do you want for them?

What will you *do* with them?
CREAAACKKKK
Secret project.
CRACK!!!
CRASH
Fifty ingots, it's ***yours***.

TUG
Well, that should hold for a bit.
Guess I'll see you.

A SECRET PROJECT?
I'VE **GOT** TO SEE.

CHAPTER 2: CORO

POOF!
Well, if she's going to leave the *door* open...
Whoa.

FOOOSSHH
HUH?
HELLO, YOU ARE ENTERING AN ACTIVE WORKSHOP. YOU'LL NEED SAFETY GOGGLES.
BEEP-Bop
Okay, thanks...

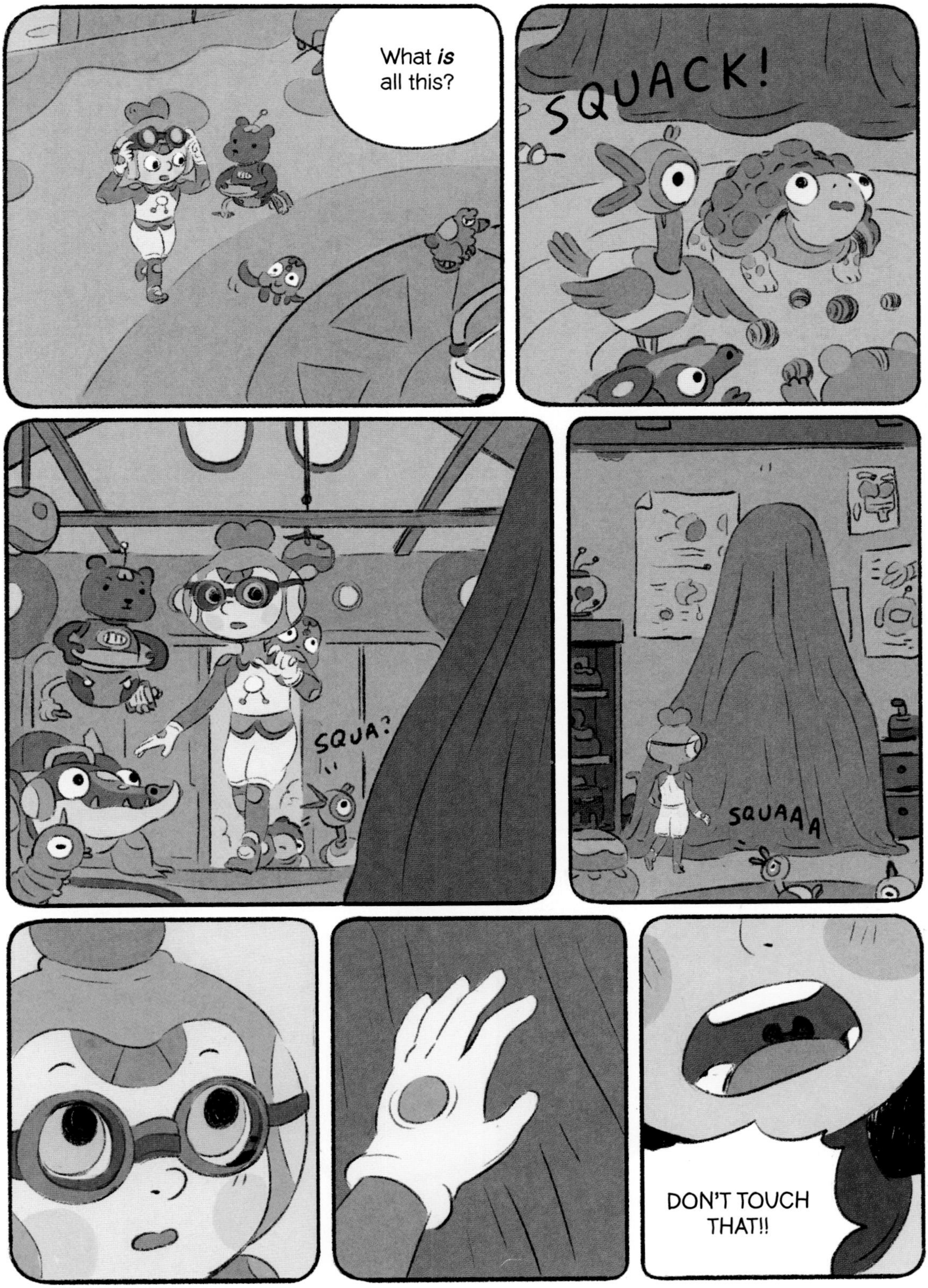

What *is* all this?
SQUACK!
SQUA?
SQUAAAA
DON'T TOUCH THAT!!

What are you doing *here*?
Oh, nothing. I just...
You left one of the OCTO-SPINNERS™.
huh
Uh, so, what are these things?
Looks like a HOVERBEAR™ crossed with a ROCKNOID™?
I made that. Sort of.
It's an ULTRA-TOY!

A *what* now?
You know how Toys have *metal cores*, just like Knights, right?
I started thinking: one Knight plus one Toy can catalyze.
ZOOT
GASP
You took its CORE out!!
So why not *two* Toys together?

But two aren't strong enough.
You're right. It takes ***three***. I usually use two Toys—
CLICK
—and a ***spare core***.
It took me a while to figure out which metals work best together.
WHOOOSH!
But I've got the hang of it now.
Zinc!
Zinc!

Chrome-
ALLOY!
Meet!
Merge!
ULTRA-TOY!
Wow.
So what happens when you ***catalyze them***?
You can't!!!

Never catalyze an ULTRA-TOY!
It's *dan-gerous* to add more power.
You can't catalyze them?
Well, *that's* dumb.
Toys are *meant* to be cata-lyzed!
It's the *best* thing in the *whole* Chasma!
Who wants a Toy you can't even catalyze?

C'mon! What were you *thinking*?
Hel-lo! Chasma to Beryl. Come in Beryl, do you read me?
Whatcha got under your ***helmet***...
Neon?
What?

I'm a ***Neon Knight***.
Oh. I didn't mean...
Don't worry about it.

I get that all the time.
Want to help me make a new Toy Cart?
I would *love* a new Toy Cart!
CORO'S TOYS
Great. Because I need someone who can fly.

CHAPTER 3: FRIENDS

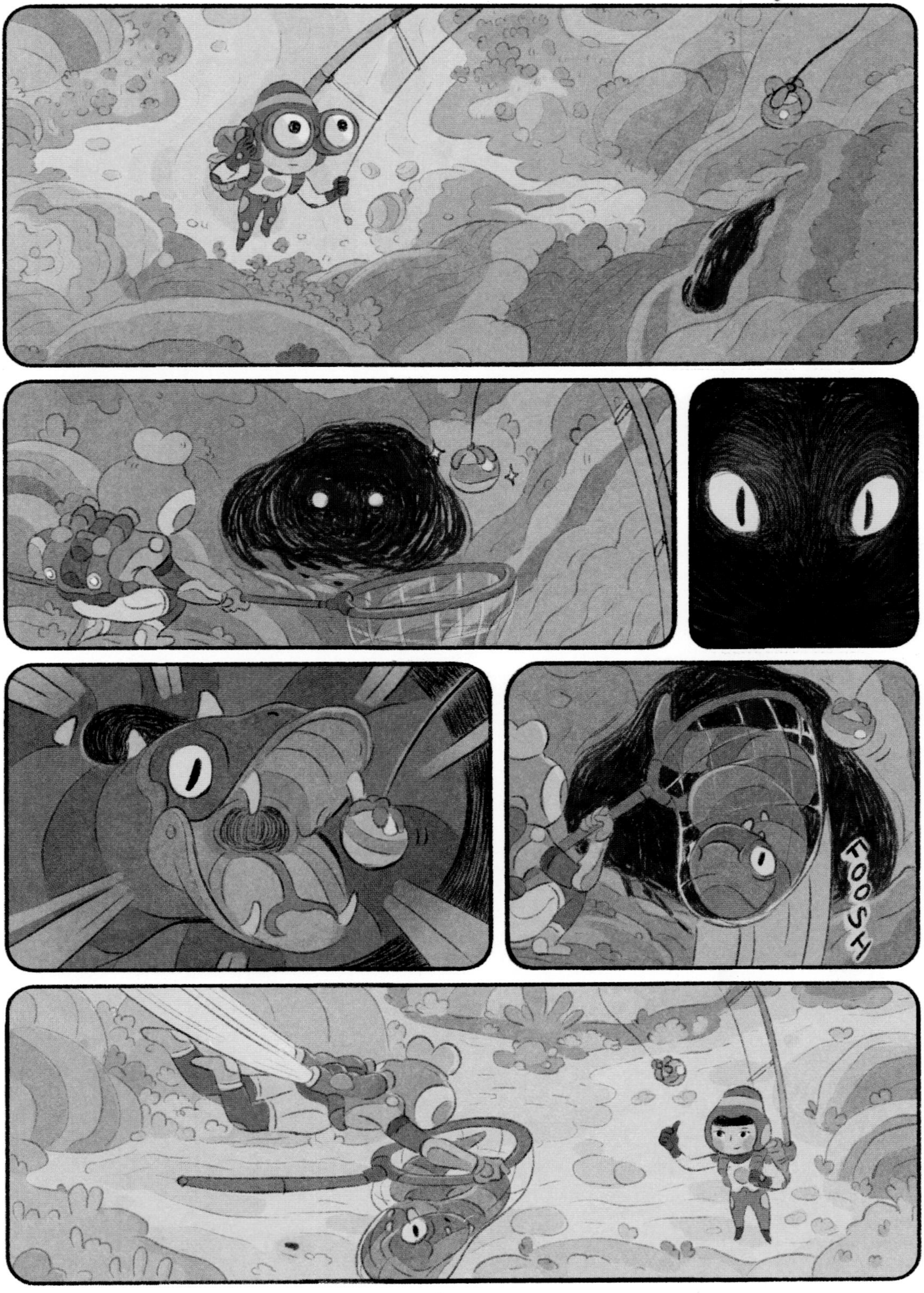
FOOSH

sqush
oOhhh

Hey! I remember when *everyone* had these.
Watch *this*!
he he he
tickle tickle
WOW!

Can you **believe** all of these cool Toys!
Why do Knights throw so many away?
They're not even **broken**!
So now...
How do we make a Toy Cart?
We've got to **figure it out**!

Just a *little* more...

Z Z Z
!!!
Of course!
Why didn't I think of it *sooner...*

Z Z
Z Z Z
WHIRR
Z Z Z
WHIRRRRRRRRRRR
CLANG!
Wha? Whozzat?

TOYS OLD and NEW CORO and BERYL
Whirrr
Ready for a *test run*?

I figured it out. It needs a gold core.
I was going to use this for my secret project.
FUUT
TOYS OLD and NEW CORO and BERYL
But that can wait.

TOYS
OLD and NEW
CORO and BERYL
FOOOSHHHH
All right! Time for that *test run...*
Coro!

I ***told*** you. ***Never*** catalyze an ULTRA-TOY!
But ***c'mon***!
We're going to the ***Toy Market***!
It's too dangerous.
But what's everyone gonna think?

Everyone is going to be so impressed—
You don't understand!
If I get there and my Toy Cart ***doesn't catalyze...***
I'm afraid everyone will ***laugh*** at me.
I didn't know you were ***afraid*** of anything.
Everyone is going to be impressed...

TOYS
TOY MARKET
...you can trust me, Coro.
TU TU TU
STOP
Excuse me.
Um—***excuse*** me—

Coro! What's that?
TOYS OLD and NEW CORO and BERYL
Hmm?
I'm *so* glad you asked.

TOYS
OLD and NEW
CORO and BERYL
Ohhh
It's my brand-new, one-of-a-kind, never-before-seen *Toy Cart*...
" WHOA "
I call it CORO'S ULTRA-DELUXE CART™!

Wow! Show us how it works!
" SO COOL "
WOW

TOYS
OLD and NEW
CORO and BERYL
The sign is Helium Bug, lit by LIZARD-LAMPS™.
OOOOOOOOOO!!!
And it's got GATOR-GRIPPER™. Very sturdy!
AAAAAAAHHHHH!!!

It's powered by a GOLD core! ***Very rare!***
And ***this*** is what happens...
OLD and NEW CORO and BERYL
...when it ***catalyzes***!
!!!

THEY'RE GONNA LOVE THIS!
GOLD!
OXYGEN!
RECOGNIZE!

she's gonna be ***sorry.***
MEET!
MERGE!

CATALYZE!

TOYS
OLD and NEW
CORO and BERYL
? ?
HUH??
SSSS
SSSS
Another Coro demonstration—*failed*!
VMM
VMM
MMM
MMM
MMM

MMMMMMM

TOYS!
OLD and NEW
CORO and BERYL
Boom
POOT
TONK!

HA HA
HAHAHA
HA
HA HA
HA
HA-HA
That's what ***show-offs*** get!
HA-HA
HA HA
HA
HA
HA HA
HA
HA

I *told* you, Coro.
Never catalyze an ULTRA-TOY.

This is all *your* fault!
You and your *dumb Toys*.
Well, who would have guessed...

A Toy breaks, and *Beryl* shows up.
Beryl shows up on broken Toys like RUST.
HA-HA
HA-HA
BROKEN BERYL

i'll show them **broken**.

CHAPTER 4: BROKEN
ppt

WHO NEEDS *THEM*?
CHEEP
I'm going to make my *own*...
...ULTRA-DELUXE-SPECIAL-WHATEVER Toy Cart™!

IF **BERYL** CAN DO IT, I CAN.
IT'S GOING TO BE **AWESOME**.
THEN BERYL WILL BE IMPRESSED.

HELLO—

WOW!
So *this* is Beryl's secret project!
What happens if I...

there.

E
AAANN
EEENNNNNN
EEENNNNN

I KNOW, I KNOW, "NEVER CATALYZE AN ULTRA-TOY."
BUT I *GOTTA* TRY THIS.
OXYGEN... ZINC...
CHROME ALLOY!
MEET!
MERGE!

ULTRA-TOY!
FOOSSHHHHH
SCR
AEE
UM...

FFOOOSHHHHHHH
I'M SO **FAST**!
!!!
...
TOO FAST...
!!!
...
EEK

OKAY, STAY IN CONTROL...

BANG!
BERYL, YOU GENIUS!
THIS IS SO AWESOME!

this is so ***awful***!
CHOMP
AAHHHHHH

WOOO!!!
CHEEP
GUU
FFOOSHHHH
FOOSHH
TWEEE!

So I said—give me that Toy, or else!
AHH!
EEK!
What is that?
SCREEEEE
No idea...

BERYL'S PROBABLY STILL AT THE *TOY MARKET*...
help
helppp
Ahh!

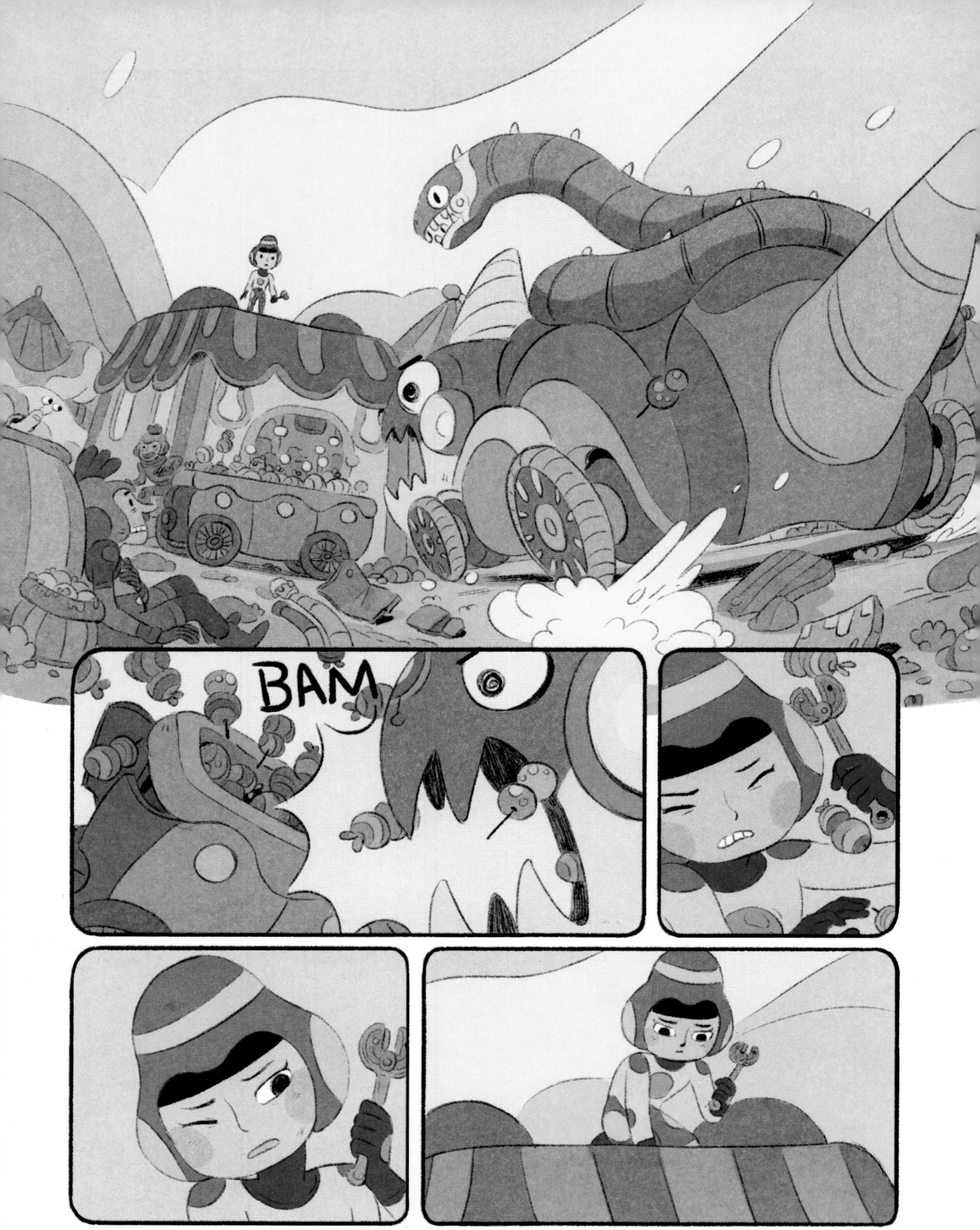
BAM

GOMP!
NOM
NOM
if i can just *pull out* the gold core...
okay. one...
two...
three!

!!!
RAWR
AHH
ARRGG

EEEEK!
BERYL!
WHAP

HUH
What—
!!!
My ULTRA-SUIT! *It works!*
Can you carry me back up?

KRRRRRRRR

whoa.
Coro?
How did you...
OXYGEN, ALLOY, ISOLATE!
SNAP! SPLIT! SEPARATE!
?? ??

Take it off!
Take it *off*!
whoa
I made this suit for me, and it's ***never worked***.
But ***you***...

I can't even get you out. Your oxygen bond is ***too strong.***
!!
HUH?

LOOK!
GASP
SWOOSHH
OXYGEN! ALLOY!
ULTRA-WRECK!
SNAP, SPLIT!
DISCONNECT!

That was so *awesome*!!!
How did you *make* that?
I worked on it for a long time.
It's not *really* broken, is it?

Did you all see that?
Did you see the ***monster***?
Did you see the ***superhero***?
That was Coro! Coro ***saved*** us!
WO OW
No.

Beryl is the hero. She made this.
She can make anything.
And now she can help us fix up the Toy Market, good as new!
? ?
Fix it?
? ? ?
Aren't we just going to buy a new one?

CHAPTER 5: MAKERS
Let's get to work!

So when you connected the gold core, it catalyzed with the copper...
Right, and blew them both.
...is the suit *ruined*?
But we can fix it, I bet!

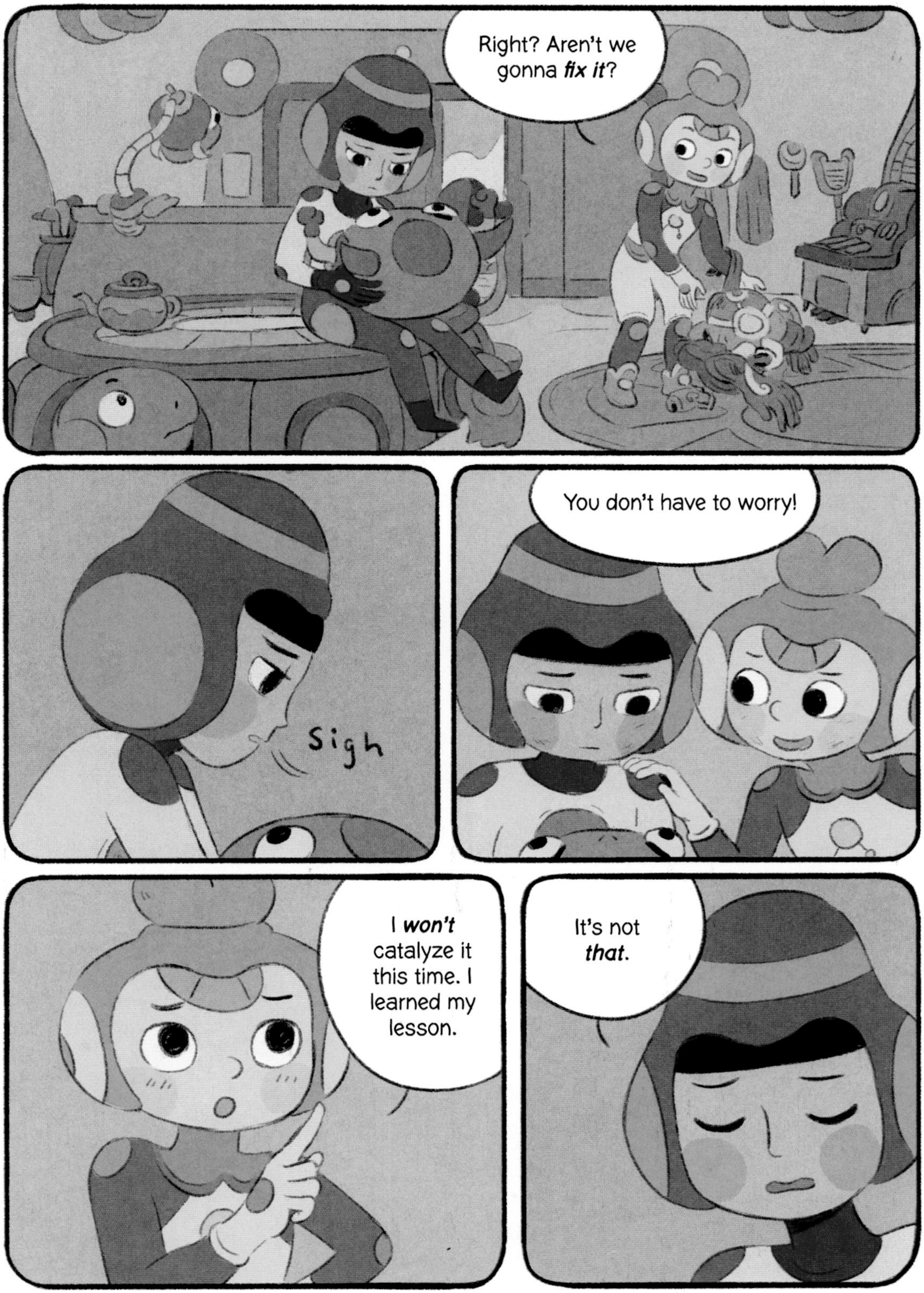
Right? Aren't we gonna *fix it*?
You don't have to worry!
Sigh
I ***won't*** catalyze it this time. I learned my lesson.
It's not ***that***.

I'm *never* gonna catalyze, am I?
I'm never gonna be *anything*...
But a *Neon Knight*.
OOF
That's why you're upset?

Who cares!?! ***You built*** all this awesome stuff!
Look.
OXYGEN! ALLOY!
RECOGNIZE!
MEET! MERGE!
Ffff
Fff
CATALYZE!

TA - DA
All I can do is turn things on.
But *you*...
You're a real, live ***TOY MAKER™***!

PUT PUT
HE HE HE HE HE
everyone in the whole chasma knows, neon knights can't catalyze...
HA HA HA HA

but wait till they see what we *can* do.

the end.

Authors' note

The original idea for the Chasma was to create a world where toys are a part of every aspect of life. (The MEOWPACK™ in chapter one was one of Boya's first sketches.) From the beginning, this world has been rooted in both imagination and its twin, invention.

As we built the idea into a story, discussing it over many afternoons in coffee shops around Baltimore, it evolved and grew, and the importance of invention took greater hold. Even though the world of the Chasma was filled with so many shiny, fun toys, there was still something missing. We wanted to create characters who didn't merely consume, but rather who were an active part of the magic of creation.

As Beryl and Coro both know, it's a joy to create new things and to take things apart, figure out how they work, and recycle them into something better. And in the process, as we figure out how to make things for ourselves, we often find that we have everything we need.

We hope these ideas are inspiring to our readers, children and parents alike, who know there's more to life than buying new toys.

Thank you for coming on this journey with us!

—Boya and Kate

BERYL

Core material: Neon
Hometown: Chasma Ring 7
Occupation: Engineer & Inventor

ULTRACRANK™

This patented Beryl tool can quickly and cleanly remove the core from any Toy in the Chasma.

POWERGAUGE™

Beryl's patented gauge instantly detects any Toy's core material and power level.

Catalyzing strength: ○ ○ ○ ○ ○
Catalyzing Toy power: ○ ○ ○ ○ ○
Toy control: ○ ○ ○ ○ ○
Stick-to-itiveness: ● ● ● ● ●

CORO

Core material: Oxygen
Hometown: Chasma Ring 7
Occupation: Toy Seller Extraordinaire

TOY

Catalyzing with Toys is the most fun thing in the Chasma.

HELMET

Always ready for daredevil flights, Chasma Knights wear their helmets all the time!

CORE

The material of a Knight's core drives their powers of catalyzation.

Catalyzing strength:	● ● ● ● ●
Catalyzing Toy power:	● ● ● ○ ○
Toy control:	● ● ○ ○ ○
Stick-to-itiveness:	● ○ ○ ○ ○

WHAT IS A CHASMA KNIGHT?

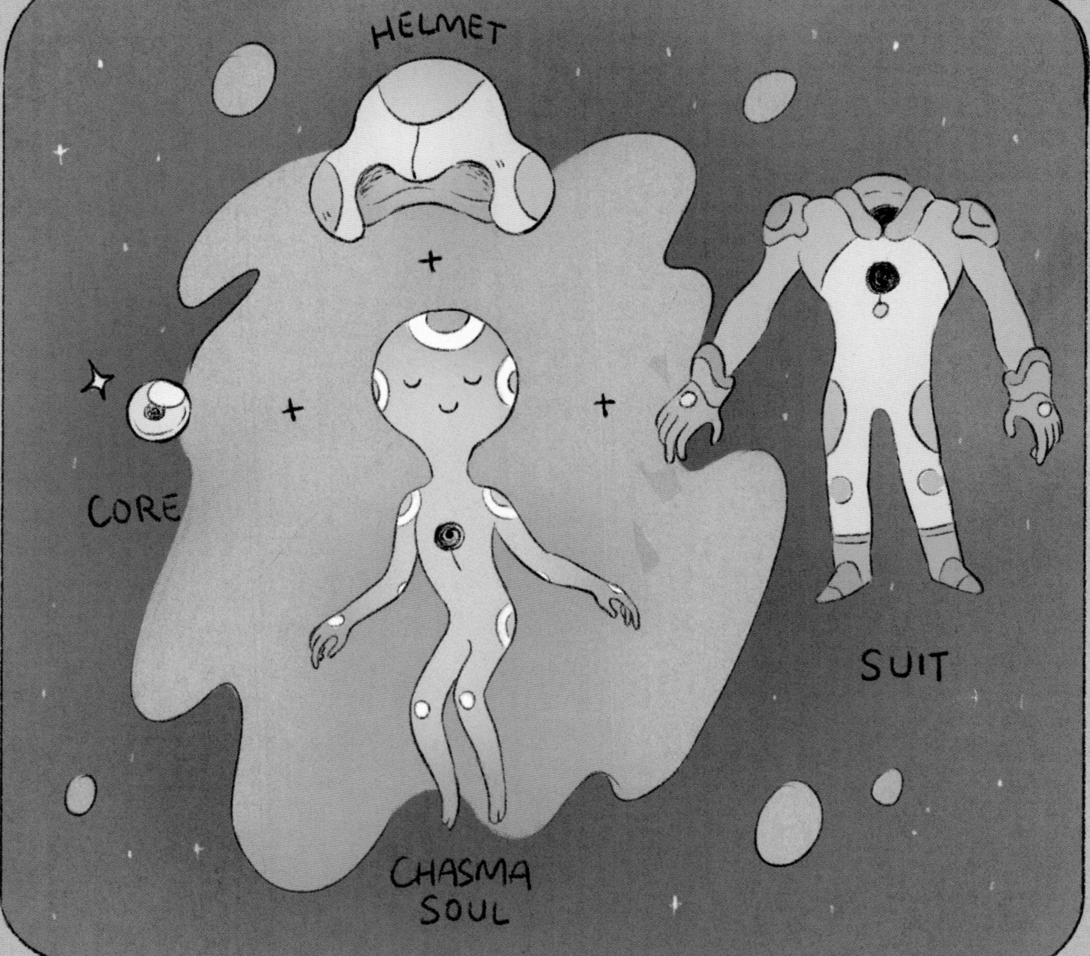

Take out a
piece of paper and
draw your own!

SOME DIFFERENT TYPES OF CORES:

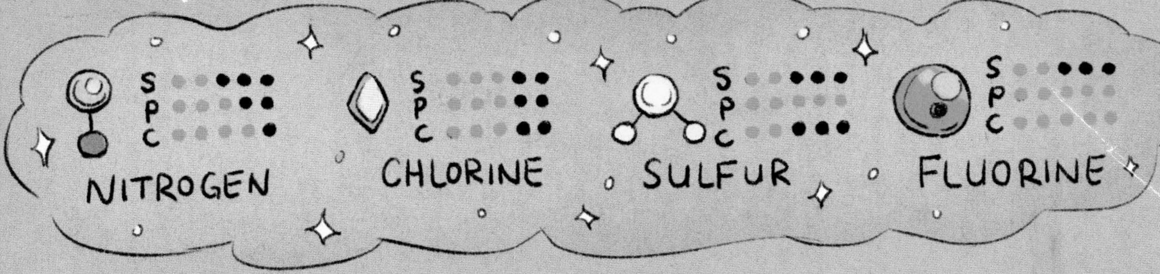

What will your knight look like?

Boya Sun

Core Material: Music
Hometown: Beijing
Occupation: Artist

Boya is an illustrator who resides in the sunny city of San Francisco. When not creating new Toys for Beryl's workshop, Boya enjoys playing random songs on the guitar and experimenting with cooking.

Kate Reed Petty

Core Material: Coffee
Hometown: Maryland
Occupation: Writer

Kate's writing has appeared in the *Los Angeles Review of Books*, *Nat. Brut*, *Ambit*, and *Narrative*. She lives in Baltimore, in a very old house that needs creative repairs as often as Coro's Toy Cart does.

Thank yous

Boya and Kate both want to thank Mark Siegel for his wisdom and generosity. And great big thanks to Robyn Chapman, Andrew Arnold, Gina Gagliano, Steve Behling, and everyone at First Second for being smart, proactive, and wonderful to work with.

From Boya:

Thank you, Mom and Dad, for your support and love. Thank you, Gigi, Pop-Pop, David, Irene, Seong Eun, and Ellie, for your generosity and for being a second family. Thank you, Cynthia and Audris, for help with the coloring. Thank you to all my friends who read the story and encouraged me along the way!

From Kate:

Thank you, JT!!! Thank you, Clementine, Frances, Zoe, Tommy, Katie, and Danny, for story feedback and new ideas. Thank you, Mom; thank you, Dad. Thank you, thank you, thank you, Oliver.

First Second

Chasma Knights is based on an
original concept by Boya Sun.

Published by First Second
First Second is an imprint of Roaring Brook Press, a division
of Holtzbrinck Publishing Holdings Limited Partnership
175 Fifth Avenue, New York, NY 10010

Library of Congress Control Number: 2017946146

ISBN: 978-1-62672-604-8

FIRST EDITION

First edition, 2018
Book design by Boya Sun and Andrew Arnold

Printed in China by RR Donnelley Asia Printing Solutions Ltd.,
Dongguan City, Guangdong Province

Sketched, inked, and colored on a Wacom Cintiq Companion 2
using Adobe Photoshop CC and graphite textures.

1 3 5 7 9 10 8 6 4 2

BY ART WE LIVE

TK